# RUDY AND TOOTY THE POO CHOO TRAIN

### A STORY BY
**Geoffrey Hoffman**

### EDITED BY
**Zachary Seibert**

### DEDICATED TO
**my wife, Allison, the best mom and grandma I know**

### FOR
**Gabriel**

Hi there! My name is Rudy.
I like cars and trucks and planes.
And most of all, my favorite is,
I love to play with trains!

The moment I wake up each morning,
I think of my trains all put away.
Tooty, my best pal, is stuck in a box.
"Time to stretch his wheels," I say.

So, gently, I lay down the tracks in my room,
linked up on the floor end to end.
Now Tooty the Train has somewhere to run!
Look! He's steaming around the bend.

Now Tooty the Train was chugging along,
when Rudy felt something strange...
like something was moving around in his tummy.
He thought, "Maybe it's time for a change."

"Oh no!" cried Rudy, clutching his tum,
The pressure was building inside him, down there.
Tooty assured him he'd wait for more fun.
"If you have to potty, you know where!"

"I think I can make it," Rudy thought to himself,
and imagined a good potty stop.
There was not much more time, and he thought he'd be fine,
but his belly was tied in a knot!

Just then something caught Rudy's nose,
And he sniffed wondering what it might be.
Tooty giggled, and said with a knowing look,
"It's stinky, but don't look at me!"

Rudy kept sniffing and whiffing the air,
asking, "Where'd that odd smell come from?"
Tooty just giggled, and tooted again, and said,
"Rudy, it came from your bum!"

"Okay, the pressure has gotten too high.
I'll be right back — goodbye!"
Holding it in, he forced a big grin,
feeling proud and a smart little guy.

Rudy stopped, and stood up from the floor,
and dashed off, as quick as could be.
He got past the door – just a few inches more –
to the potty where big kids go pee.

He turned around quickly, pulled down his pants,
and sat on the potty with glee.
He thought, "My diaper's still dry!" as he let it all fly,
"I went to the potty to pee!"

Then Rudy noticed he wasn't quite done,
but there was nothing to dread.
That's when he remembered this excellent tip,
something his daddy once said:

"There's two kinds of stuff, that come out of us,
and both of them smell kind of fishy...
Pee is yellow and slippery and wet,
and poop is like brown goo, and squishy."

Rudy heaved a breath of relief
and sighed, "I'm almost through!"
But wait — there's actually a couple of steps
I have a few more things to do!

His tummy rumbling and face turning green,
He pushed one more time without doubt.
"Hey Mommy, I did it! My poo's in the potty!"
then he shouted, "Come check it out!"

As soon as I'm done, I have to clean up
and wipe myself front to back...
if I still see grime, then wipe one more time,
No sticky ick left in my crack!

18

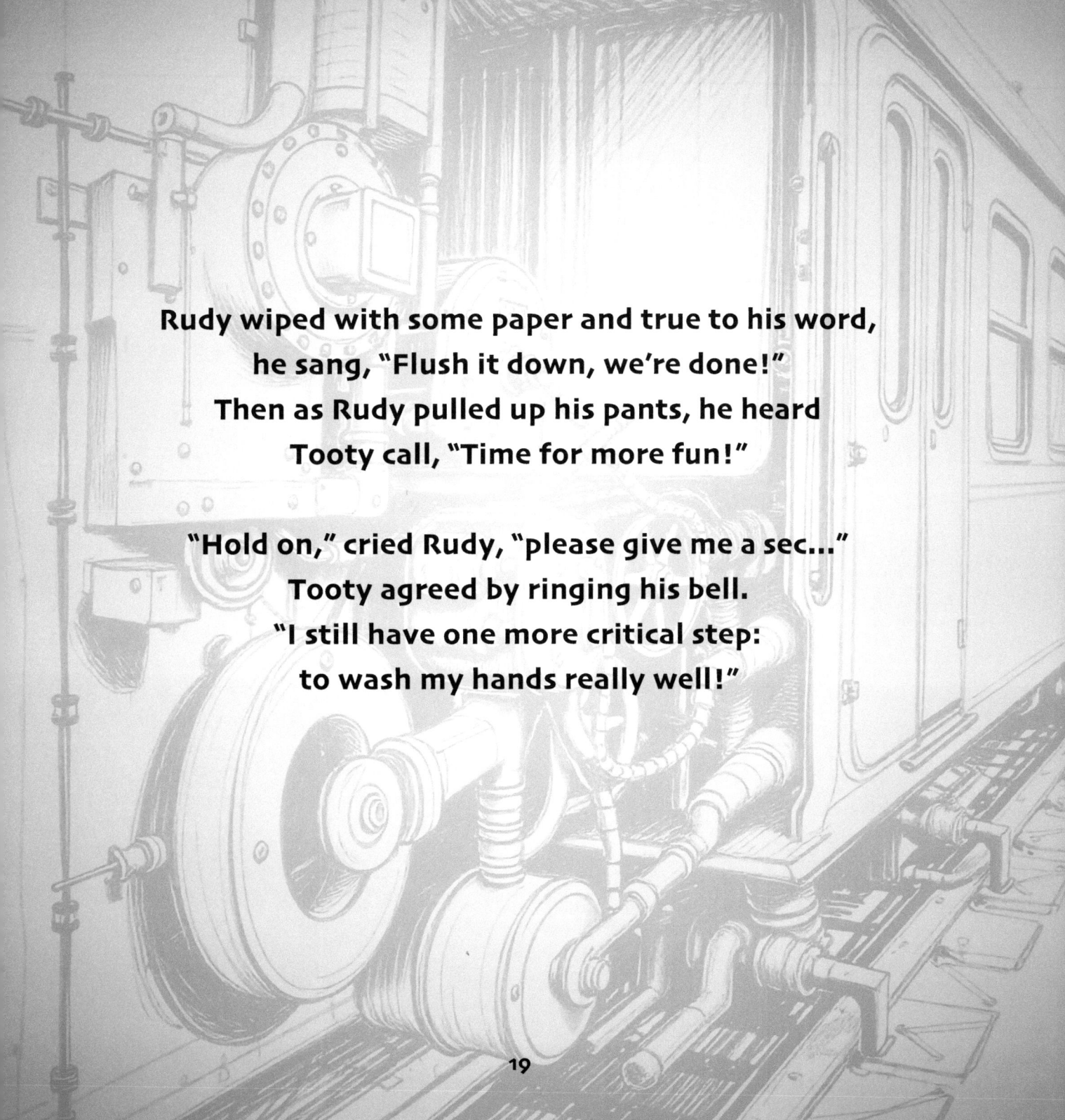

Rudy wiped with some paper and true to his word,
he sang, "Flush it down, we're done!"
Then as Rudy pulled up his pants, he heard
Tooty call, "Time for more fun!"

"Hold on," cried Rudy, "please give me a sec..."
Tooty agreed by ringing his bell.
"I still have one more critical step:
to wash my hands really well!"

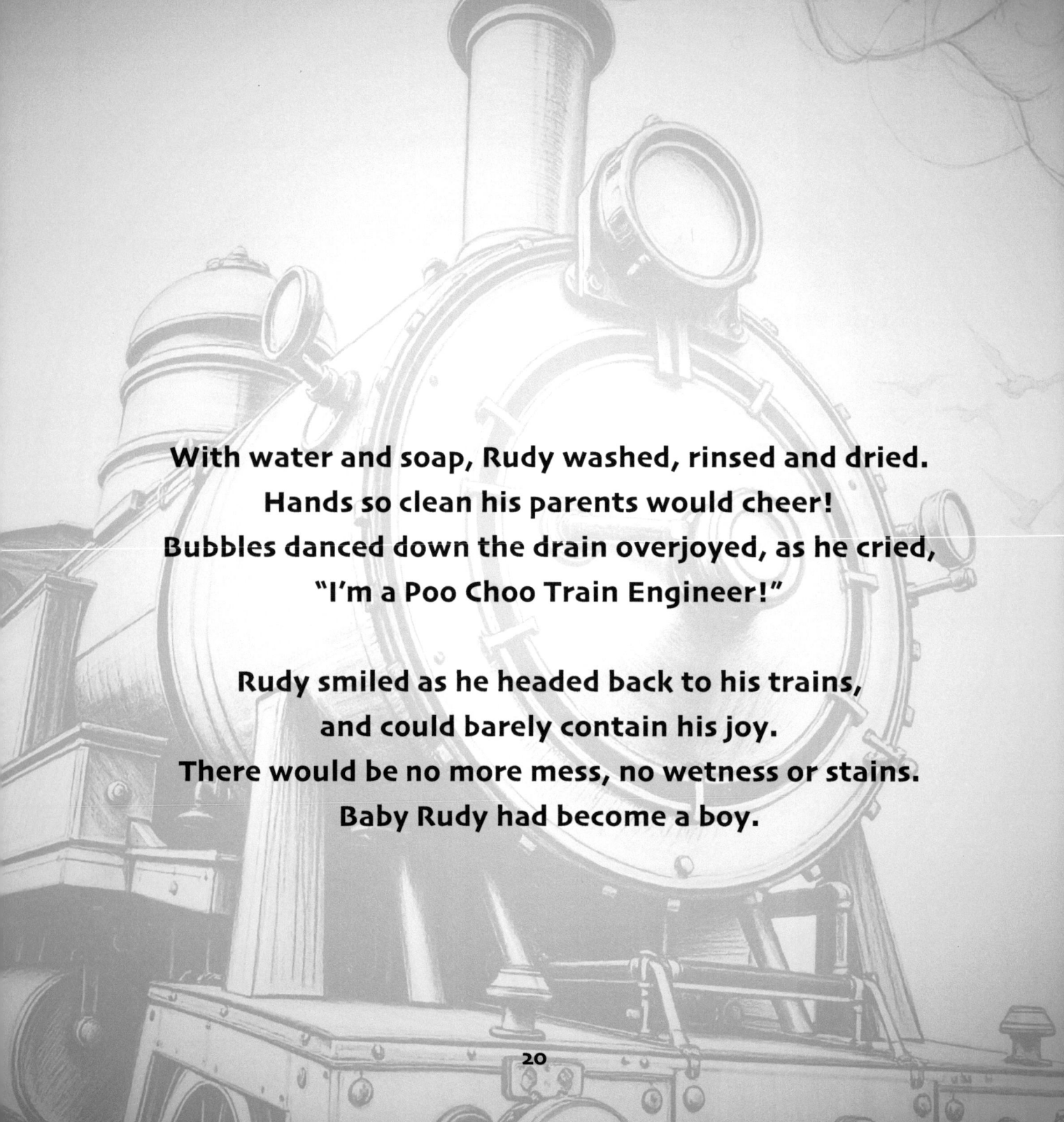

With water and soap, Rudy washed, rinsed and dried.
Hands so clean his parents would cheer!
Bubbles danced down the drain overjoyed, as he cried,
"I'm a Poo Choo Train Engineer!"

Rudy smiled as he headed back to his trains,
and could barely contain his joy.
There would be no more mess, no wetness or stains.
Baby Rudy had become a boy.

21

"Now that I'm back on my potty train track,
There will be no more diapers for me!
If I can do it, then I know you can too!
Try it next time and you'll see!"

## RUDY AND TOOTY
## THE POO CHOO TRAIN

For more adventures with Rudy and Tooty, visit RudyTootyBooks.com